I0741936

IMAGES FINALLY FOCUSED

by Young T. Hughley

No man can have a harlot

for a lover

nor stay in bed forever

with a lie.

He must rise up

And face the morning sky

and himself, in the mirror

Of his lover's eye.

From James Baldwin's "A Lover's Question"
JAMES BALDWIN JIMMY'S BLUES AND OTHER POEMS

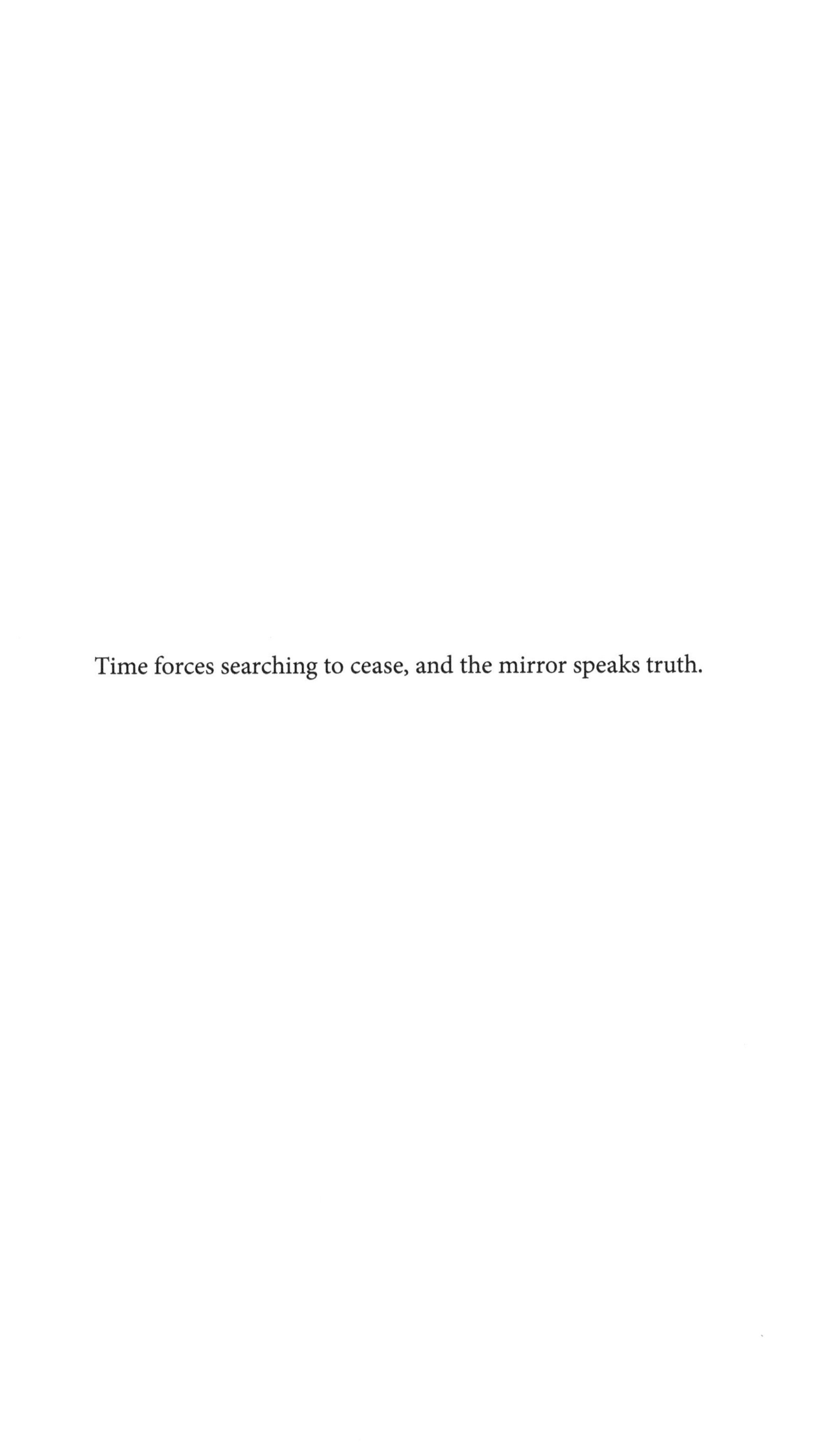

Time forces searching to cease, and the mirror speaks truth.

DEDICATION

I dedicate this body of work to my sisters; Antoinette, Annie and Jennifer
who came to my first reading and embraced my efforts. To the memory of
Louise C. Smith and Maggie D. Carter, two beautiful women of color, both
played the role of godmother to me and nurtured my sensitivity because
I needed comforting. My parents Y.T. and Mamie Lee Hughley who had
eleven children and learned to love each for who they are/were. To my
brothers and sister, who during a most vulnerable time, taught me what
family love and acceptance is all about.

INTRODUCTION

Reflecting on the words in this book the theme of suppression and triumph came to mind. I also came to realize that there are others who grew up in a culture of suppression and who still struggle with their authenticity. I am in awe of the new generation who live in a much more tolerant and expressive time. Some, occasionally not understanding those who still struggle with labels and identifying. My hope is that one day we all will embrace inclusion and acceptance, understanding that people are born to be who they are. My prayer is that the poems, short stories and essays in this book will add to the discussion that will enrich our community. Please enjoy these expressions by a Heterohomo who grew to love himself. I wish happiness and strength to all as you explore life and hope that you find peace in your being.

Table of Content

Life's Short Poem # 1

Innocent touches arouse.

Simple smiles ignite a glow.

Scent of familiar bodies

in houses, form humans.

Hums and hugs wrapped in

Blissful kisses

Infancy starts

Journey

Alpha to Omega.

Life's Short Poem # 2

Creators on blank canvases

confident or unsteady,

self-taught artisans

flourishes with brushes;

sensitive palates,

construct life voyagers.

BEFORE NOW (Pre-the revolutions; civil & gay)

Before:
Dr. Spock
Affirmative Action
Equal Opportunity
and Stonewall.
Boys were to be jocks
Girls trophies
Children seen,
Wives floor mats.

Everything had a place;
white was right until
slave became nigger
Became colored
Became Negro
Became Black
Became African American
Became Afro-Eurasian
Became you pick…

Religion ruled with stars and stripes
virgin births and resurrections on the third day
Nothing but THE blood could make you whole.
Innocence knows, but dare not say,
"There is no virgin birth,"
Nor is all America beautiful.

A boy yearns for a doll
perfunctorily chooses the gun.
The girl loving pants forced into pink dress
not wanting to disappoint
Feminine side subdued,
Masculine potential booed.
Wanting…to be held and touched,
Forbidden….
No cuddles or caresses
TEARS wrapped with duress.

Maternal eyes speak
FOR GOD'S SAKE, EMBRACE THE ROLE.
Be…
like your father
your brother
your sister
A Beauty Queen.
War on the home front
mama Judged
daddy's not responsible
for
The unspeakable!
The curse!
The disease!
Explaining to family and friends
The Jewel Box Review the boy would do,
Grease monkey girl turning a screw.
Labeling God's Creations
Sissyfaggirlyman,
Dykemanbutchwoman
WASTED if Not married!
Blameless ones denied
his femininity
her masculinity.
Beloved Community
Dream killers before they killed
Martin Luther King.

There are no pots filled with
GOLD
at the end of gay rainbows.
Slayers of Personhood,
misguided guardians
adapting scripts from hijacked lives
parents' hypocrisy, aka
history repeating itself.
Automatic spouse. Automatic life.
Automatic child.
Before the revolutions, before now.

"NORMAL"

Thank God for THE AGE of fast forward
The Miraculous VCR with Difficult INSTRUCTIONS
DVRs that allow us to stop, start, and repeat.

Technology at the speed of light
dropping Tsunami waves of information
wisdom that frightens or enlightens.
Humans are creators, improvisers, unique,
there are no owners' manuals for children.
Diverse sexual and gender expression is common
In all cultures.

Children should be allowed
to be who they are:
LESBIANS, GAYS, BISEXUALS, TRANSEXUALS,
HETEROSEXUALS, BI-GENDER.
All Queer!
All Dear
"Normal"

Life's Short Poem # 3

Remarkable beauties awaken the heart

encounters that burst like a new dawning

Out of dormant earth.

Feminine Brilliance, Brawn Magnificent

curiosities of wonder.

"What creatures these mortals be?"

And I Loved You
(*Age Seventy* reflects on a Romance at age fifteen)

You called me names that made me shame,
no matter what you said I was the blame
and I loved you.

At 15 years, an innocent lad,
too young to know his object of
Affection was a cad.

You lied to me which I believed
you talked to me and I heeded
and I loved you.

Man-child searching,
a wild urchin
missing hugging and kissing.

You loved me and I enjoyed it
you mistreated me and I employed it
and I loved you.

An English assignment gone awry
Miss Proctor loved the rhymes that day
not aware lost boy could be prey or gay.

You loved another who broke your heart
you came back to me and I mended the parts
and I loved you.

Surprised poem made front cover
young boy hovered over mimeographed journal
hoping that no one knew his lover Ronald.

You went away and I cried
you came back my eyes were dried
and I loved you

Youthful anxiety needing sobriety
sexual and emotional exploration
Headlines high school's publication.

You made of me a golden rule
I was happy to be your fool
and I loved you.

Death may come and take me
But all I care and know is that I loved you
and I love you.

Defining moment set in sex, life hurled into a vortex
self-love the journey came to be
today proud to say that boy was me.

AND I LOVE ME.

My Poetry

My first attempt was to explain my poetry to myself.
why?
WHY?
I didn't read like others? Did not sound like others?
Vocabulary was not like others?
Till the old man I used to hate, Said
"Stop, it's yours, it's you, It's exclusive…
God's uniqueness is expressed
In the likeness of us Humans"
Yes,
I thought,
HER way of giving us a kiss
Firmly holding us with both hands.
HIS assurance with a smile
Pushing us forward
Whispering in our ears…Do you.

It Will Never Leave You

It's wonderful to have.
But you can't have It if you don't believe It.
Your inner voice.
It tells you that you are beautiful.
It informs you that all does not happen in a day
and that darkness won't be always.
It explains the emptiness of this place
Void of you.

You, obsessed that your nose is flat, cheek bones sit too high
Butt too big and your calves don't accentuate
the perfect flow from your thigh, ankle to feet
which are too flat and too big!

It sees the genius in you, opportunities not won
given or maybe taken
and still has great hope for your tomorrow.
It tells you that all is perfect.

Barely make it through your day
starring in your own horror film,
hungry zombies at your heel.
You, comfortable in a film noir.
It gives you two thumbs up
five stars and a free pass.

Nothing is wrong with your hair
your smile can wait on bleaching
you needn't make worry a profession
It tells you.
Despite that, you dig up garbage
all about yourself that should have been tossed
Incinerated
buried years ago.

When despair rages; a soldier in combat
braving enemy fire, It will fight for you.

Sees victory around the corner
at every turn, lifting you to your next level.
It dreams dreams for you.

Your peers dump you.
While watching you reconnect with the crew
that deserted you and will
again,
It promises to never ever leave you.

Quietly it sits and waits, hoping that one day
you will notice sadly knowing
It can't live in your life unless You Believe.
It will never leave you.

Your essence beckons
With words of adoration
Encouragement
It loves you more than you know
Be willing to trust it
Believe it.

Stuck on Scarlett and finding Bow-Dollar

There she was bigger than life on the huge screen at the Lowes' Grand Theater where she premiered twenty years earlier to an all-white audience in a segregated theater. That day I was sitting in the mezzanine, my choice, because of equal rights.

Her green eyes captured me as I watched her in the barren fields of Tara. She stood there as the sun set or was it rising? She raised her fist to the heavens and declared that she would never be hungry again. If she had to steal or kill she would never be hungry again.

It was one of those major promotions on TV and in the papers. Anybody who wanted to be anybody and in the know, had to see the film. At fifteen I wanted to be somebody. I wanted to be in the know and cultured.
I was dressed in my good clothes. It was the Sixties. Downtown Atlanta businesses were gradually integrating. To represent I am sure I wore slacks, a Sunday shirt and maybe a suit jacket. The occasion was the 20th anniversary of the film Gone with the Wind or perhaps it had been re-mastered in the latest technology. Bow Dollar; aka Robert Lisbon, secretary of our social club, The Friars, was in tow.

One of the guys in the group gave him his nick name. Lisbon kept talking about his "bow dollar" collection. As a bunch of teenage boys, we were curious. One day, while at his apartment in Carver Homes where we lived, he took us to the bedroom he shared with his brother. Out of his drawer, in the chest shared with his brothers, he took a sock out. It was filled with coins. We laugh informing him that they were silver dollars not bow dollars. "My dad called them bow dollars. That's what they will always be for me."

His mother had given them to him as a reminder of his father. I can't remember if his dad was dead or just not in the home. The guys chuckled and someone, within our midst relating said; "Ok…. Bow Dollar", dubbing him with that name from that day on.

As a man of color I have never been comfortable with my secret loving Scarlett O' Hara. She is a Shero of mine. My first encounter with her was at the movies that day. Later I explored her deeply in Margaret Mitchell's book. She epitomized femininity liberated, not female liberation. I was aware of strong women, like my mother and other women in the community; but 'Miss Scarlett' radiated like a delicate flower, manipulated like a black widow and operated like a damsel in distress to conquer. What Power! It was later in life that I realized how conniving.

My teenage mind marveled at such wonder that was so outside the world I knew of women. Scarlett was different. Anna Lucaster and Porgy's Bess started this fascination for me; liberated females. Women who did not let men or circumstances define them. At an age when I was evolving emotionally, sexually trying to determine my 'spectrum of maleness' these women were appealing. They defied domination and classification.

I don't know how I convinced Bow to accompany me. He was a sleepy-eyed dude who liked basketball and football. He was thin of frame and could be perceived as sickly. The high school band was his lot by default. We both played third chair trombone and were bonding as buddies. I know I convinced him to attend the film. Today I realize it is something that he never would have gone to on his own.

At fifteen I found things in the movie that connected me with Scarlett. I forgave her for living on a plantation. I understood the vastness of the geography and the politics of plantations, I lived in public housing. Her father was crazy, an Irish land owner who liked to drink. As a teenager, I had come to realize that my father was crazy, a hard-working poor black man who liked to drink. I understood universes out of order, crazy daddies, not enough money or food to eat.

Contented slaves on the verge of freedom comforting white folk didn't set well with me. I could understand them whining like babies; having been slaves all their lives, not knowing what to do with this possible moment of liberation. The only flaw in the movie that day as far as I was concerned. Slaves whining like babies, okay; but trying to maintain their place with southern decorum, ridiculous!

The anguish of being hungry: scared, insecure and having you be the only thing holding IT together, I understood. That lone figure etched in an orange hue with dark purplish clouds looming in the background, standing boldly, bigger than life on a gigantic movie screen: a smidgen of dirt on her forehead and cheeks; fragile but strong.

It was clear to me it was not a prayer. it was a declaration. She was just like me, careful not to denounce the existence of God just in case. Angry enough to raise a fist and exclaim why was this happening to her and me. Why were we stretched to the edge of our emotions in our worlds; hers' falling apart; mine for the last 15, going on 16 years marginalized by segregation and poverty? I determined, like her, that once I got control I would never be hungry or poor again. Oh yeah… I would always have the land and if I could not solve it today, I would think about it tomorrow.

Turner Classic Movies 31 days of Oscars brought me to place. Why do I stop, whatever I am doing when this movie is shown on TV? Why did I bother to read Rhett Butler's People? As a black man, I had to ask myself why I liked Scarlett or the movie Gone with the Wind. Bow Dollar is no longer with this world. He died young for a grown man. My thoughts of him have been far and in between. Happy that at this moment in trying to understand my fascination with Scarlett his memory comes to call. A smile on my face knowing that he would not have chosen that movie but braved it with me anyway. Wondering if Lisbon, my friend, had any idea how I was taken with Scarlett that day? I don't recall us discussing the movie - ever. The ride back to Carver Homes was on a bus system, newly integrated. People still self-segregated. Not comfortable sitting next to people not like them.

My junior year in high school I used the S. O'Hara method; garnished with my masculinity, to conduct my high school political campaign to become President of the student body government. Bow Dollar took first chair of the trombone section in the band. I would like to imagine that Rhett Butler might have been his influence. Nostalgia tells me that I should relish the fact that he was a friend; willing to accompany me to an integrated movie theater in the new south watching me, watch a film about the old south and that our bond of brotherhood survived that.

The Order of Maya

Cupid blows can make one bleed.
Emotional intercourse
done with the wrong person
can lead to loneliness wrapped in madness;
some strange people disease others
call crazy
caused by some greedy mongrel without
pedigree.

Those who gnaw at kindness
pigs at troughs
vultures cleaning bones until nothing left
rodents nibbling at vulnerabilities
droppings scattered in sacred places
joy crumbled for sports.

Amorous adventures should not require
full Armor, guarded and cumbersome!
If one must venture into
the theater of love
go as gladiator in the order of Maya.
The soothsayer Angelou
knew
why caged birds sing and
hurt people hurt people.
Her words Carved in your shield,
" when someone shows you
who they are believe them;
the first time."

For Anonymous

I thought it was time I sat and wrote about you,
to express the trivia two hearts love and laughter can experience.

This is a birthday gift, if you save the paper It might become an antique
My first effort to say…I LOVE YOU.
To describe the feelings EASY, GOOD, SECURE (Oops, I slipped with
words).

Exploring hands, happy. Moving sensuously from heads to toes to mouths
to sexual
organs
Hot steaming wet bodies proclaiming fantasies and Insults
me freeing me on you …in you Letting go of emotions
and you Yours …in me… Screaming,

See me, see me…only to laugh and radiate all over

To share the secret, we knew each other from the beginning
and loved US
You, you
Me,
Me.

Un Bel Di

"You are in for a treat" the best friend shrieked,
that he had never entered the red painted door off the busy street
or climbed the stairs to ecstasy. Admission paid by Membership.
Ravenous seasoned veteran proceeds with emancipated appetite
while the novice left alone explores directions to erections.
100% cotton white towel wrapped.

Camphor scented mist like vapors roasting men in heat filled rooms;
arranged meat on smorgasbords for grazing fills the hunger
in the dark where days and nights are hidden. Men dish choices explored
with hands
a feast without camaraderie yet demands.

Brushed Encounters, faceless silhouetted manhood's displayed.
A gentle tap with guiding motion to tub of hot bubbly water
where strangers chat with aliases; nervous laughter,
brief exchanges in passageway, ménage a' trois,
orgasmic orgy, whispered words of nothing true.

Men frolicking in wading pools. Beautiful bodies stretched out on towels,
wet or dry, vanity certain of its physique. Lust and love tango with his
heart.

Opened eyes inform him the dance is solo. This is not what he expected.
Dreams don't become realities in a bathhouse.
Unfulfilled wishes remain in this chamber of brief encounters,
soiled towels discarded lust left in hampers
mildew bound.

Dressed, His feet lead him to the street,
home to Butterfly
Puccini's style.

The sweet voice of Leontyne wraps him in the desperate warmth.
Slumber comes all alone heads resting; one gently caressed by his
hand between his thighs, the other on his arm cuffed in an elbow.
"Un Bel Di" his cradlesong.

Life's Short Poem # 4

His and Her stories

Egos, hopes and passions framed
creating tales of optimists

Pessimists

Glory seekers......

Witness bearers to others
wiser, stronger, broken

All Repositories

SELF-SCULPTORS

The First Step in The Journey

My vision is not as good as I thought
Nefertiti is in mourning
Seeking solitude somewhere in her darkness
A page from Vogue or Harper Bazaar
All Nebulous descriptions.

You are more woman than I think
Or you want to be.
When all minds and desires are equal maybe we can talk;
Postponed the postpone, forever seeking truth.
Femininity or masculinity is that the question
Or is It more our ability to cope?

Emotions are toys, Women snigger with a ruse,
Men pretend with reason. Blinking lights are approaching
in the distance.

Truth has yet an expanse to traverse; meanwhile Pleasure, Praise
Fame, Gain, Pain, Disgrace, Blame,
and Loss; Constants in life.
My vision is not as bad as I thought
WE chose to forget the work, WE conveniently lost Interest,
Truth is Feeling all things that are felt
When taking the journey
Into KNOWING.

Jenny Is a Bitch!

Jenny is a bitch sacred witch,
the Bible her sword talking with a twitch
about fornicators in Leviticus
Adam sleeping with Steve, Eve with Weaves.

Jenny is a bitch went wild with her 7th …year itch
bound for glory anyway.
Brother's gay she curses the day
some man swapped his swagger for a sway.

Jenny is a bitch, enough of her tricks.
Comforting sisters whose husbands have split
In the name of Jesus, she counsels Mary in her bed
Joseph is not the end-all; he can sleep in the shed.
Control him forever, keep the baby, no maybe.

Jenny is a bitch, Hypocrisy helped her dig a ditch
The hole so deep at night Jenny weeps.
Her husband is a bore
She wants him to sleep on the floor.

A double life lived, the other down low
Jenny hurts; a life filled with woes
Fighting her fascination for vaginal glows.

That's so Gay!

Most of my life I felt alone
hiding lies as companions to mask reality.
A self-imposed mugging that robs us of our joy;
life lived with aspirations cannot be wrapped
In Self-delusions and
Denials.
Sometimes the light is fearsome,
but I prefer that terror rather than
the prison admiration.
Life and visions are experienced best
thru self-ownership of all that is you.
You can lose or win in life.
If that's so gay, so be it!

My straight friend wants the word gay back

He said he wanted it
returned to his straight world.
Word hijacked by a minority
My good friend explained.
A term no longer could he use
To express gaiety for things.

"Straight people don't say they are straight!"

Do I tell him it was a better choice
than faggot, pervert or queer
At the time taken?
Do I say "the straights" labeled us first
with terms, unacceptable
abuses and asylums?
Do I tell him once upon a time
a people created a community
called it gay,
Affirming themselves?

Uneasiness,
Boxes and labels.
No one owns the word
he can use it
wherever, however.
We'd all rather be called by name,
Known for who we are.

Now
That I have removed
My Mask, not feeling the need to
Man-Up to be in his presence
Do I Silently enjoy his frustration
for loving me

Perhaps the question is his.
Why my proclaiming my pride
a part of me
Disturbs him so?

Life's Short Poem # 5

An invincible thrust of force

Orange, yellow, purple and metallic grey

variegated twirls

adorning broad leaf moments of trust

Dangling strong,

while winds, rains, sun and pestilence

beat at its glow.

Shielded by sensations of hope

Rooted in understandings

that have no visible ends

with constant beginnings.

44

He Had Done No Wrong

The day he announced God departed;
"Gone fishing in an undisclosed location,"
his church family prayed in tongues
Deacons rebuked the devil
Mothers' of the church wailed and lamented
spiritual brothers and sisters danced
banishing demons in their midst
The minister preached "the wrong men do."

He felt dressed in sackcloth covered with ashes
Loved Ones planned their lives
casing themselves in righteousness
and prays to Jesus for tomorrows
Without him.
1986 the year of the sentence
HIV invading temples and leaving ruins
Medicine men of the new world
had no hope.

Through this Valley of the Shadow of Death
The Deities of his forefathers
The Christ of Darkest Africa
And the Light of Illuminations
Would warp the force field of his planet
He danced a Pende Mask edged in kuba cloth.

Nail fetishes, to some eyes, eerie wooden carvings
placed about the rooms
Small burlap sacks tied tightly
Containing potions
that would confine the virus.
Nkisi figures for those who know
on the mantelshelf
Tall village marker rounded with three heads
Top to bottom, spike driven nails anchoring future germs
And infestations
Guard the entrance to the kitchen
with sacred blessings written and hidden

in dust cover boxes sealed with glass
Power figures to stop the plague.

Water, herbs, vegetables
Revered flesh
Grapes, apples, melons of all sorts
Sea weeds from darkest black to lightest green
Eaten with hope of healing
Deeds to be done,
LIFE till DEATH!

His body vibrates, the ritual begins
Palms meet awaking thunder
Prayers to all Gods who will hear
Not a sinner, a man flawed and good.
He had done no wrong.

Coupled

They sit watching the sun set in the west
An unanticipated breeze wraps both bodies
in a coolness, not man made
fireflies dance in the dusk
The evening stars shimmer glow unnoticed
like the secrets of their hearts

Silence binds the two, chatty no more
emotions wrapped in pain killers
as two hands void of feelings touch
Laughter belongs to a creature neither knows
politeness masks the years of shared intimacy
lost in lies, entrusted to other, exchanged for careers

Two souls seated, a splendid vista
each familiar with the other
tongues tied
one sighs, the other gazes
The wind sweeps by like the 23 years
NOT Getting to This Place
eyes connecting two strangers
unaware with awareness

Silence like mosquitoes beckons for departure
smiles cured in concrete on each face
they rise embracing the other's regrets
Love leads them to walk home alone
coupled

STRANGE

I'm just learning to love you
I did all the time, I think?
Pseudo liberalism, individualized man
My woman at my side, not my back
Un-Possessed! A free spirit…

My actions
were dictated by others' expectations.
My reflections in your eyes
were of a real world
that goes on with or without you.
Proprietorship unnecessary
Friendship essential, honesty everything.
I am learning uncertainty
when explored, embraced and PURGED
is healthy.

Mysticism mixed with cries and whispers
If I listen
I hear you, shaken now (close to fragile)
Connecting you in me
Getting stronger
You are a part of my soul
Strange……I'm just learning to love you?

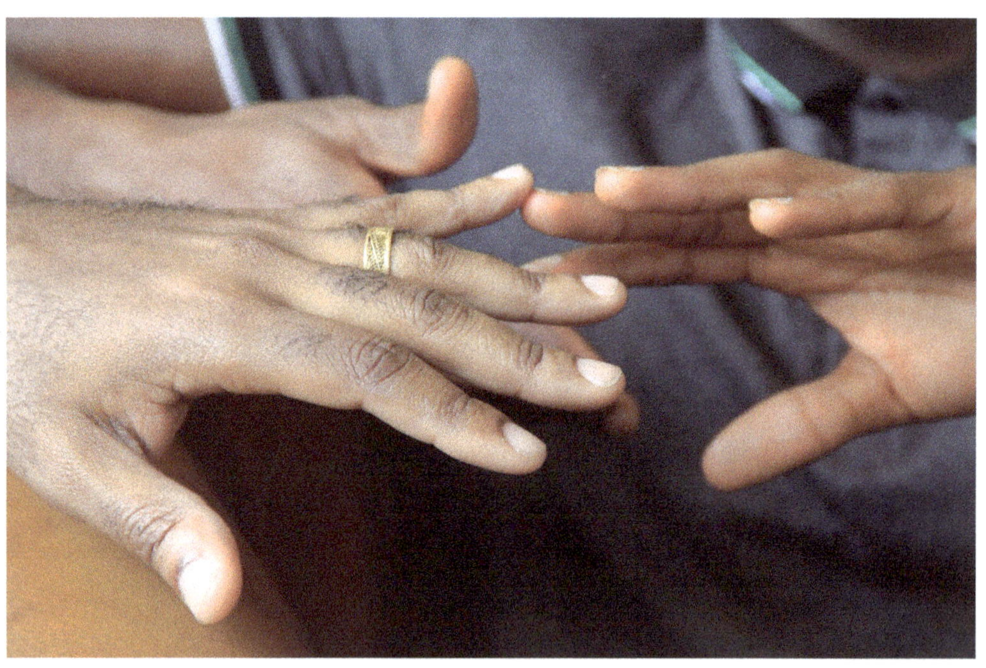

A Condensed Journal on the Search for Mr. Right

Gladly abandoned my emotions, before they were ready to be freed, needs for a moment met; eyes, arms, calves, these physical features in other men were more suited to my liking. The desire to find Mr. Right led me to this quest.

I searched for him in a red bone man, biceps sculptured, green eyes. A Man of mad passion who fought for love brutishly with hard stained hands from working on cars; that brandished knives which left sexy scars and pain that hurt. His nights flowed with melancholic moods that paralyzed and blues tunes without lyrics.

Hollywood confused my search. Life was too big in Panavision; romances too beautiful in cinemascope; conflicting my reality. Men off screen never said the correct thing or held me the right way. The glow from street lamps never captured their radiance. Images of my leading man was footage left on cutting room floors; black Adonis whose dreams are lost to daylight and monster when nightfall.

Throughout life my search took many shapes and forms. Mr. Rights were found in a college lover who made himself indispensable until he conquered; an elderly gentleman preying on young lads, giving them their wants and desires 'til he was satisfied and on to other prey, recruited by his throwaway lovers; all a cast of young men needing love, affirmation of their secret, a daddy who cared, a sense of belonging, sad; trying to find themselves.

Passive aggressive love intertwined with surrender and defeat made a great fantasy, a way to play until age dissolves the pretend. I thought I had found Mr. Right in a young man lost in time. Kings conquering Kings, Emperors… Emperors, enjoying great battles of sexual conquest without commitment; rulers of worlds carved out of illusions. Maturity intruded on my manhood and I embraced life's realities with a desire for something more than sex. Compromise no longer an option.

In my mother's eyes, I often looked for him. She knew him well and experienced unknown adventures and maintained secrets of their union foreign to me. A merger created out of contented love that was not enough, fused with too much and too little of nonsense, deceptive games, pain of rejection, on the same search as mine, enduring till her death, taking the secret of what little she knew of Mr. Right with her.

Time forces searching to cease and the mirror speaks truth in focused images.

I found him in a body ravaged by cancer, numb with morphine and needing comfort. Death gurgles blended his consciousness with mine. He whispered, "You won"; wrapping him in my arms I replied, "It was never a game. Who cares about winning?" The gurgle took his breath away and peace sat between the two of us launching the final link.

Parents never love us the way we want. They can only love us the way they know.

I am the love of my father as he knew it, visions of the future he could never imagine, aspirations denied him and his hope to one day get it right. I am his restlessness in the search for self and love; comfortable with the imperfections in both, and the certainty of knowing, that I know, when I know that I know. He is in my dreams of family that can never be, and a family that is. The wondering eye as I look for someone to love, to love me. He is in rooms I don't occupy anymore and muttered speech meant to be forgotten. I see him in the way I chew my food and smack my lips. He is there in my indecisiveness when uncomfortable; my nervous laughter as my voice trails toward silence. He is enfolded in the joy and excitement I hide from the world to maintain my coolness while exploding at my body's core.

Mr. Right is found in the fullness of me and all my mistakes. He is all that I have and all that I am willing to give. He is the love that I know and the love I am willing to receive that will make me more than I was before. I am Mr. Right!

Like the Phoenix

Up from ashes out of the self-mutilating fire
I hear Yemoja's song.
Her power cleansing melody releases me
from a living death.
Bayard Rustin and James Baldwin are my heroes.
Like Kunta Kinte, I must be called by my name.
I am a proud African American man, gay.
Liberated from darkness into a fulfilled life.
I am a baby boomer glowing in the security
and warmth of all that makes up the person of me;
no longer a perpetrator
in this universe on a planet called Earth,
located in: the western hemisphere,
residing in a neighborhood of my choice,
on the Continent of North America
in the USA, State of Georgia,
the city of Atlanta
where the phoenix is always rising.

Life's Short Poem # 6

Bellies bloat, Breasts slope, Shape Changers

tenderness to sustain,

bejeweled expectations managing

shadows of anger.

Eternities wrapped in words fortified with embraces

for days that will get better.

(…. In Search of Meaning)
The Call

Are you asleep?
No, he says. Time says differently.
Waking gives him voice as gulps of air
stimulate his brain to readiness.
Covers rustle long distance
I see his body floating
on the ocean of mattresses
that often entertained our fantasies
and only of late our hearts.
Why do you lie?
Framing it in a chide,
wrapping it in a bow
knotted with a tease
wanting truth;
aware of the time of night,
morning searching for daylight.
Hoping that he knows
it is Ok to say 'I was asleep'.
Instead
"I'm here" he says
to reassure, "Happy that you called".
Silence mingles with distant endearments
barely audible…,
"babe, you my stuff, of course I care",
from that place where he lives.
Go to sleep, I say, as sudden as a night
owl's hoot;
pressing the off button
gently on the landline
as if it were a kiss upon his cheeks.
A quiet quaking within me,
Seismic waves at the thought.

Why Won't Love Stay

Do you ever wonder why love will not stay?
You are on the same vibe
Heaven's door is open wide
It is the best day of creations
And
Love just gets up and walks away.
Do you wonder?
Why won't love stay?

The day is filled with laughter and joy
Orchids, roses, Nature is blooming
Lifting you and yours into a
Utopia euphoria
And
Love walks away.
Why won't love stay?

You just created an App
Wealthy beyond dreams
You are mother father husband wife
Honey baby sugar sweetheart
Best friend and lover
The most exciting thing since……
And love walks away!
Why won't love stay?

I look at you; you look at me, eyes on each other
Adoringly
WE are Echoes resounding and dreams bouncing off the walls
Conquering Mount Everest
Hiking the Appalachian Trail
PERFECT WEATHER

Your brother, your lover, your wife, your husband, your partner
Everything is in synch
Intellect loving Intellect and stupid loving stupid
Tears so sweet that you could just die today
And

Love just gets up walks away....
Leaves the room we occupy
Why won't love stay?

Perfect sunset, a full moon,
Blinking stars dance in the universe
No mosquitoes, summer night cool breeze filled
with magnolia scent,
A sense of mother's love abounding
You
Full of good self without Ego
An unbelievable exactness
Then one of you, like a Brilliant being on Crack,
Questions some banal nonsense
And
Love just gets up and walks away.
Why won't love stay?

The Magician

Like a magician doing disappearing acts
Puff
Vanishing in thin air
Reappearing
In unexpected places
In a *flash*
The cover of a cloak
Over fragile bodies sewn in half
Stitched back together with the wave of a wand
Love thrives in the mystic region
where
Imperfections are made perfect
Kind acts disappear, realities clash,
Enchanted moments are created
Disappearing, clashing, re-creating
Over and Over Again

The Discovery

He will bring fragments of shard glass
and mine-field promises from past
attempts at relationships;
confident and certain of their importance
not bitter
wiser and tougher.

Her song will bellow like
penitent sinners
monks chanting for redemption
an angelic choir pleading for
atonement, providing
sweet melodic days that fold into
nights, strengthened by hope of works
unseen.

They will maintain old relations
faux and diamond speckled moments
infinitely treasuring them; as they explore
depths of hidden treasures within themselves.

He will rejoice; inspect and behold
imperfect and rare gems;
old and new maps that connect
soul mates with
the Oneness of Worlds
in existing galaxies filled with cosmic
phenomenon.

Her passionate soul, a geyser
in territories unexplored by pioneers;
too certain and unprepared
for glacier reflections of
beings shivering jubilantly
with trust and joy in the
unfamiliar.

She will not be looking for a way out.
He will not be attempting to move up.
Neither pretending to be something they are not
Nor wanting to own what's not theirs
Both responsible for what they bring.
Happy explorers dwelling on the intimacies
of their journey to the discovery.

Life's Short Poem #7

Gratitude glows with each breath

trailing the moon and sun

season after season.

Death anchoring impermanence

hours; minutes of lifetimes

irreplaceable years

hinged with tears and laughter.

Hallowed.

NEEDING COMFORT FOOD

No one fries fish like my mother. She fried whiting fish perfectly and make the best cold slaw. That is all I could think about as I attempted to quiet the need for some form of satisfaction trying to evade a feeling of rejection.

I hate fried fish from fast food places. But there I stood at the counter of Seafood Haven because of my need for …comfort.

The service counter was clean and the first person I notice behind it, to the left, was a thin chocolate sister with Beyoncé hair. She was happily manning the drive-thru window. The kitchen was staffed by a soul brother.

There was no question that he was "The Man" in the house. He ruled the deep fryer and lorded over the prep counter and the women. Standing before me was a large dark skinned woman with a beautiful smile. Her canine teeth accented and trimmed in gold on both sides of her mouth. I dubbed her my counter hostess and soothsayer; she knew I didn't know what I wanted.

"Take your time" she said as she continued stocking the containers on the counter with plastic utensils, condiments, napkins, etc...
I stood there disappointed that I would have to settle for foam like patties of white fish meats compressed; pretending to be fresh fish dipped in foreign batter nothing like my mom's. I knew that the tartar and hot sauces my hostess, was restocking, would provide the essential flavors for my taste-buds. The perfect camouflage for food that could only be found in my mother's kitchen. I yearned to bring my evening to a pleasing conclusion, something beyond vagueness.

"I will have the fried white fish meal".
"What sides do you want with that? You get two."

She looked to be thirty-something with kids. While I was trying to decide, she started texting. Her maternal authority blended with the worried look on her face formed ridges around the corners of her mouth. The hard lines traced deep into a visage where it was not yet time. Between placing wrapped utensils and stuffing the proper sections, she texts like a mad woman. Once certain that whatever directive she sent out was not challenged, she gave me a smile and a nod of her head to proceed with my order.

"Broccoli and green beans", I said slowly hoping the vegetables would negate the greasy calories I would devour once home.

"And to drink?"

"I am trying to be healthy here."

"Then you want the smoothie" she said thanking me while taking my credit card, "Your order number is 316". It shouldn't take long."

I placed my credit card away and gave myself permission to look about the place. It was my first time in the West End.

This Seafood Haven was small with several tables for guests. There was a family of four and a couple on a possible date. It was late so I imagined we were the last of the customers for the evening. This made me wonder why the wait.

The door flung opened and the gush of air exiting the building drew my eyes toward the entrance. A younger man, handsome, in his forties, with a soiled handkerchief tied around his head like a bandanna, entered. His tweed suit jacket looked expensive, dated and worn. A sweater vest covering a shirt collar that seemed frayed from days of wear and tear. His complexion was a smooth bronze brown. I used to think black men of that complexion were really hot. The stain around his collar gave me pause. It was from body sweat and perhaps a lack of washing. Handsome and homeless was my read. Jeans completed his outfit with tennis shoes that trended many fashion years past. I saw a striking figure altered by adversity. A state I felt was new to him. Our eyes met; me conscious of staring, embarrassed, turned away waiting for my food.

There was a swift change of energy in the place. Silence crept in like a cockroach at a formal tea. The staff was busy with work. The happiness, the lording and the gold trimmed smile were stuck somewhere between my order and the door opening. Dining conversations, that were hardly audible, became whispers. I turned to look into the room where customers ate. Their movemet was as played in slow motion on a video. My eyes rested on the bronze brown brother. He was digging through the trash where customers discard their garbage when done eating. Destitution and hunger were visible in the room and nobody wanted to see it.

He looked at me looking at him. Gawking, I was now certain he was handsome beneath his despair. Intuitively, I felt he was also educated and at one time promising. Not to write him off completely, I surmised that he still held promise for his mother if she was living and not deceased like mine.

He held back the swinging lid of the trash can with his left arm. With the right hand he took out bags and clumps of discarded food. He placed them on the side of the container on a used service tray. He examined his findings; carefully looking for portions that could make a meal. He placed a jumbo cup with the lid off on top of the container. He filled it with left over cups, of liquids, found in his dig. Food that others had declared waste would provide nutrition for his evening and perhaps start his morning.

That fear came whispering 'there but for the grace of God go I'.
From my lips and someplace warm grounded within me came these words, non-judgmental wrapped in polite inquiry, "What are you doing?" I was surprised at how naive I sounded and how stupid the question was. Men don't dig in garbage unless they are starving!

He looked at me with that look of unbelief that I couldn't see the obvious.

Are you hungry?" I asked, cutting to the quick.
"Yes" poured gently, honestly from his lips exhausted.
"Put that back", I whispered as a command. "What would you like?"
brought back the muted sounds of food and chatter and halted the embarrassing moment in its tracks. Life resumed at Seafood Haven.

He stood there puzzled for just a moment then stepped up like the prodigal son invited to the banquet. He surveyed the menu on the wall.

"You can have anything you want" I said unclear what prompt my generosity. Was it the bronze brown complexion? No, it was not. It was about the humanity of a man; the journey of two travelers dealing with life as it was dealt.

"I will have the catfish feast"

The mother in the hostess informed him as was her job;" Which sides? You have a choice of three."

The young girl at the drive-thru giggled at some comment over the intercom. The cook in the kitchen hummed a tune that I didn't know while we all waited.

"Corn on the cob; broccoli, mac and cheese, one large ice tea, please," he said completing his order.

I gave the woman my Visa. She checked me out. The cooked yelled "316 is ready!"
"Will my guest be ok?" directed at my hostess.
"Yes," said smiling; pleased at my deed.

I opened the door to leave, the suction formed the air pocket that created the gush of wind as before. The stranger turned to watch. Our eyes met connecting us. "You're set."
"Thanks," he said sheepishly waiting for his number to be called.

The frustration with my writing and the glorious volume, to be, of poems on life; love and affirmation had lost its sense of urgency. That moment with someone that I may never see again had lifted me. My gratitude and gratefulness for what life had givenme, provided me nourishment. On my drive home I no longer needed comfort food.

Homage to Dawning

Two white winged Doves at the feeder;
a small house, kaleidoscope painted contraption
tin roof covered in tar
(Remnants from a barn in Alabama, I was told)
hanging
from the rafter on the porch.

From my living room window
I watch birds come and go;
people walking and cars passing
none appearing attentive to the day
the beauty of the morning lost in their haste;
to catch a bus, beat the traffic
obsessed with living making.

Mortals, walking, driving
Thought once tadpoles, wiggly things, apes
Humankind
Flying creatures, winged things
Perhaps once dinosaurs?
Evolving
now; birds feeding.
Me
Hominin Clade
Having my morning coffee
Thinking of Langston Hughes' "STILL HERE".
Not plague-consumed or ravished by aging
Bio clock ticking
Progress.

A Cardinal comes to partake of the feast
The doves take flight,
reminding me of many no-longer here.
Transition.

Sipping the brew that connects me to the day;
peacefully observing the blazing red coat
adorning the feathered visitor,

68

Surprised by unexpected guests;
Blue Winged Warblers traveling farther south
to places unknown to me.
My mind bobbles briefly on a journey to be taken.
Comfortable with Uncertainty
I celebrate the morning.

Grace

Thankful that joy was the last to kiss me before I slept.
Morning to peace which greets me as I rise.
Showered in gratitude, embracing grace, thankful
for the Pass to live the day in each moment
without anticipation.
Walking, talking, serving, and eating,
breathing each second soundly…
thankful to get to sleep, perhaps again with
joy.

Life Short Poem # 8

Winter winds wrapping wisdom in

Memories; sorrows and joys

ornately dressed.

The sage finds center

grasps each day with no regrets.

Forgiveness a gift to fools

wise ones choose Carpe diem

the body speaks

bones, organs, muscles, mind

compete.

The Act

Some moments are strange to me
A worldly man of understanding
Finality is certain
But some days my heart yearns
For a nod or smile
From the one person I expected
To adhere to the chronology
of life
who still occupies a space in me
filled with needing:
Compassion
Caring
Forgiveness in Abundance
all unsolicited
all unconditional

I stand here sixty-five and counting
new day more precious than the one before
accelerating minutes at some point freezing
into unexpected seconds of reminiscences
expressed in
A simple act
That can't be performed anymore
Picking up the phone
Dialing
Listening to the ring tone
A voice never distant regardless
Inhaling/exhaling
Sacred chant like salutation
"Hey Baby"
A Psyche providing Comfort
Via
Telephone Cables
A connection to my source
And I say
'Hi Mom, how was your day?'

Sister
Let her
have it she
gone take
everything
anyway
Mother
Imagine s
Imagine s
trying to
away
Imagin
We all stood in the kitchen
in disbelief as Old Mrs. was
served the peach cobbler and
boasted to her guests that
she had took over the kitchen
to make it.
Rhina

A Shotgun House!

(Autobiographical sketch of the mind of **A** black man in public)

Three rooms connected one behind the other
standing outside, front door to back
looks like beams supporting a tunnel
straight line leading into caverns;
one for living, sleep in another,
cooking and eating in the third
with all doors open
shot from a gun
could go straight through,
provided no one was in its path
front to back, day or night
a shotgun house his dad said.

No more than four in 1950
he stood there puzzled
visualized the only image known
shotgun buried deep
in the family closet
warning
'If you touch it you may die"

Dad smiled at the wrinkled brow
Eyes puzzled loomed beneath it
questioned
Why would anyone
Shoot
a gun through a house?
"People are crazy,
shoot clear through
cheating spouse
mean spirited man
unwary fools
talk too much
blameless folk
dark forces, evil intent
doors open or closed

target bound to be hit
shotgun house,
that's why they call it that.

From that moment to this
The boy imagined
his body that house
three rooms
body, mind and spirit
visible so that all could see.
Strangers deciphering passageways
that made him before he was made
Shotgun blast of words
Spraying through rooms
Front to back, doors open or closed
Target hit, enemy/friendly fire.

Boy man now (dad deceased)
writes poems from
a shotgun house.
Crafted with collected stacks of bullet casings
sealed with mortar made from gun powder
doors always open.

Life's Short Poem #9

Present and past bound round…absent vigor

consigned to urns and rituals, chambers in the ground.

Reminiscences of places in the heart;

with tears of elation shaped by grief

and hope.

Death in the Family

The life sustaining machine gave rhythm to a room where death was about to take place; could possibly take place? My brother John, two years earlier had done the miraculous; came back from the dead like Lazarus. Perhaps it could happen again… my hope.

The hospice room was too comfortable. Designed that way I supposed. There is nothing comfortable about the experience called death; at least not for the living. The only thing missing in the room was the scented candle.

At the window overlooking another wing of the building was a sofa that could accommodate two maybe three but no more. The drapes were a muted dark blue. A strange color, just enough hue to convey warmth for comfort or bright enough to give hope. Imitation mahogany panels serve as the headboard. A fitting background for the multiplex of machinery that give breath, food and alerted the staff when they should make an appearance to provide some degree of comfort, for the hibernating patient floating somewhere between life and death.

Here I am again looking at my brother on a ventilator. An oxygen tube securely fastened around his nose. My mind hums as I surveyed all who had come to witness the event. I struggled. None of his brothers or sisters were there; our brothers and sisters. Should I even be here? Why am I thinking this way?

All my brother's children are here except for a son and the eldest daughter. She gave consent and informed us all of the chosen date and time of the unexpected? The occasion; to remove the life sustaining equipment. The moment was approaching when he, my brother would determine if he would breathe on his own or give up the ghost. My hum had morphed into a counter beat to the ping of the machinery that has supported his life for three weeks.

For three weeks his visitors were family and hospital staff in and out of the room. On my watch, I spoke to the sedated body, wondering if my younger brother could hear anything at all. My sisters' experience had been that he squeezed their hands or batted an eye. He gave me no signs of life as I spoke of our past and future together. He must be hearing me though. Maybe?

My younger brother had a talent for being absorbed in something else while taking in every detail and conversation going on about him. He could be totally occupied and engaged in conversation with another; but tuned into private dialogues, being conducted, by two unsuspecting guests in a room talking quietly in a corner. Even with his body in this state John must be using this talent. I often wondered if others had picked up on his unique skill of reconnaissance? He relished telling me everything he captured on the sidebars. Did others know about this gift? His children now standing around his bedside waiting…Did they know?

Who are these people; kept clawing at my senses. I don't know them! I know that it's my brother's two sons and a daughter. I recognized the significant others in their lives. The spouses, flawed like all spouses. Three handsome grandsons, ages 5 -12; yet to determine who they will be with or without their grandfather. An assortment of supportive well-meaning in-laws, who liked and did not like my brother depending on the issues or circumstances.

There was also a stranger who had 'heard of the event' and wanted to be present. John had been influential in his life and supportive. I took the hand proffered by the young man upon meeting him in this room for the first time. The irony of the moment for me: grasping a sorrow in him that I did not know; 'now you want to support him in his death', nodding my head politely but not speaking those words. My brother was the man who sat by the side of the road being a friend to men.

Where were my brothers and sisters? That biological unit created by my mom and dad? They should be the ones with me for this event, not these strangers. To calm my inner turmoil, I declared myself a protagonist. I gave name to the antagonist to give my emotions a sense of clarity. His or her name is death.

I sit on a chair not too distant from the foot of the bed. His children formed a semi-circle around the bed but left an opening on either side not to interrupt my view. My brother's eyes were slightly closed and the life-giving tube was taped on both sides of his mouth as we waited for its' removal.

John was always vibrant. Even as he wrestled with the consequences of: too much drinking, being overweight, living hard and enjoying the numbing effects of drugs. Six years younger than me. He indulged me as the oldest brother reminding me that life was not always heavy. I have always loved and truly liked him. He has always been his "own man" as the expression goes.

Mom and dad worked at night, I oversaw the house and children until they got home. We were latch key kids before sociologist knew they existed. I saw that they had dinner, did homework, kept the house clean and went to bed at a decent hour. When needed I was the disciplinarian. The incident that bonded us was tied to such a moment. My attempt to discipline.

I don't remember the situation. I only remember the mortal combat that lead to my hands around his neck as I pinned him to the floor. My sister screaming "Y'all stop" and me demanding that he "do what I say". Tears formed in both his eyes as determination to resist screamed at me "Kill me! Kill me.... and see won't you be in trouble when mom and dad get home!" I paused from my destruction of the younger brother. My sister went silent, perhaps contemplating the consequence; that she would be held responsible if I completed the act. John found humor in the situation and burst out in laughter looking at whatever expression I might have had on my face.

Realizing the absurdity of the moment I found laughter lurking someplace in my being and rolled over on the floor beside him. We enjoyed that moment of insanity; understanding that brothers and sisters keeping house are responsible for the wellbeing of each other.

'Brothers and sisters responsible for the wellbeing of each other' made it clear who these people were. They are John's family and I am here to be supportive of them as an uncle. I am now the latchkey kid for death because I am the oldest living member of our clan. I am single, divorced and have no children. My nieces and nephews have provided me with my limited experience with offspring.

My mind settles on the sixth and seventh stanzas in a poem by Essex Hemphill entitled COMMITMENTS: "I am always there For critical emergences, graduations, The middle of the night. I am the invisible son in the family Photos, nothing appears out of character. I smile as I serve my duty."

The hospice social worker enters the room. She acknowledges that this is a large crowd for such an occasion. My brother's eldest son introduces all that are there and give explanations for the two siblings who are not. In acknowledging me he says "This is our uncle, my father's brother. He is with us."

She precedes with instructions of all we can expect as life supporting devices are removed. My brother Edwin enters the room as she concludes. His presence provides me with a sigh of relief. Shortly afterwards the doctor and nursing staff enters the room to perform the act.

I look at my brother's three grandsons. "Are you guys hungry?" Their eyes aglow at the tendered reprieve from this ceremony that they are not yet ready to experience. I see the man, that I now hear grasping for air, in each of them. I know he approves of my action. Unlatching the lever to the room that waits for death, I lead them in search of the cafeteria. My brother John loved life. The only door that he would have wanted them remembering him passing through, at such tender ages, is that of life; greeting them at his place or theirs'.

Life Short Poem #10

Lives on earth shaped by Mystical transformations;

Dust to dust the Human flesh

Hopes of reincarnation

Anticipated Heavenly reunions

Prophets Clarifications,

Peace at last

Hurts and Sorrows purged

Infinite Celestial Celebrations

Life chasing the Hereafter

Here

After Here.

Notes and Credits

Page 18, The Jewel Box Review. An African American traveling female impersonator show that toured the US in the 1950's.

Page 29, Lowes Grand Theater was in downtown Atlanta Georgia. In 1939 the Hollywood Premiere of GONE WITH THE WIND was held there.

Page 30, Anna Lucaster, a film released in 1958, starring Eartha Kitt and Sammy Davis, Jr.

Page 30, Bess, The love interest of Porgy from the opera and movie; Porgy and Bess.

Page 31, Carver Homes, HUD housing project in Atlanta GA. Present day name "Village of Carver".

Page 29, "When someone shows you who they are believe them; the first time". Quote of Maya Angelou.

Page 31, Un Bel Di, title taken from an aria in the opera Madama Butterfly by Puccini.

Page 35, Leontyne, a reference to the renown African American opera soprano Leontyne Price who premiered at the Metropolitan Opera in 1961.

Page 53, Yemoja, Yoruba Goddess celebrated as the given of life and mother of all.

Page 68, STILL HERE a popular poem by Langston Hughes, an African American Writer.

Acknowledgements:

A special thank you to all the folk who emotionally supported me on this project and offered suggestions to make it better.

John Coleman (Posthumously) I see him arguing with the creator.

Clarence White and Mitchell Watkins who read, what I thought was my final draft, and gave me encouragement.

The men in my writers' group. They affirmed, encouraged and made suggestions that helped me stretch.

A host of readers, you know who you are, you made suggestions and kept pushing me forward with candor and stimulation. My friends who would listen to what I wrote when I had the need to read aloud.

Chris Cheech and Felton Eddy for edit suggestions and observations. My dear brother from another mother Ramon Hughes for unceasing encouragement.

Duncan Teague and Simone Bell, both provided additional edits and encouraged me to release my truth to the universe.

Finally, Jean-Patrick Guichard who provided consistency and support by helping me make this project a reality and all the artist who gave permission for the use of their work without hesitation based on their trust of who I am.

About the Author

Young was born in Atlanta Georgia. He grew up public housing from the mid-fifties to late sixties. He comes from a family of modest means. There were seven brothers, three sisters plus his mom and dad in the home. If you are counting; yes, there were 13 people in the Hughley household.

Being an introvert, the library at Luther Judson Price High school became his best friend. Reading was a refuge and writing became a means of expression that was a personal comfort to Hughley.

After working his way through college, his focus was on sustaining himself and the pursuit of the "American Dream" via credit cards and the pursuit of a relationship. In his forties he realized that working to pay off credit cards was a stress additive to an already complicated life. He divorced after 23 years of marriage. Materialism was exchange for quality of life that lead to self-examination and exploration.

He has been fortunate to work in: corporate America, the Broadway theatrical arena, consult on the very first National Black Arts Festival in Atlanta, own an art gallery and lead a successful community revitalization effort in the historical African American Reynoldstown Community in Atlanta.

Mr. Hughley is proud to have earned his BA degree from Morehouse College as well as three executive certificates from Harvard University, Kennedy School of Government as a recipient of fellowships and in recognition of his community development work. This is his first book.